Conventional Short Stories

By David Evans

Table of Contents

The Sailor and his Dog

Bennie was in the Navy for twenty years and when he retired he was looking for a puppy to keep him company.

While he was in the Navy his wife passed away from cancer, he hasn't been right since that day.

Most of his family live in another state, and rarely visit him. He has one son who recently moved to Germany for his job, and sometimes calls him.

He was making a to do list and was debating if he was going to take a walk around the neighborhood.

He looked out the window and it was a beautiful day outside; the birds were chirping, and beautiful butterflies were flying around.

His neighbor was cutting his grass, and a woman was walking her dogs. That's when he thought to himself I really need a dog.

He was finishing up washing his cereal bowl and carefully dried it off placing it on the counter.

His neighbor knocked on his door, hold on I'm coming. He quickly opened the door; his neighbor was standing there.

"Hello Jim, how are you today?"

"I'm feeling just fine."

Later today I'm going to a major league baseball game with my son.

3

You can gladly come with us, I would but I'm having personal issues.

"What kind of personal issues?"

"I'm dealing with loneliness."

I'm sure that you would feel much better among people, my son won't mind you coming along.

You have to get out of here more often, I do get out every day. I really want a dog, then you should go to the pet shop.

The last time I went there they were sold out of dogs, I'm sure that they have some dogs there today.

"Do you know what kind of dog you're looking for?"

"Yes."

I know someone whose selling puppies, and I'll take you there if you want. Let's go then, you look a lot better but smile on your face.

"Do you have all of your belongings with you?"

"Yes."

Jim exited his home and locked the door behind him and walked over to his neighbor's truck.

"Did you just get this truck?"

"Yes."

His neighbor opened the passenger side door for him, he got in closing the door.

"Do you mind the windows being down?"

"No."

We should be there in forty-five minutes; he's been a friend of mine for years.

"What breed of dog is he selling?"

"Beagle puppies."

"Where's your son these days?"

"He's somewhere in Germany."

I can tell that, that really bothers you. He needs to come and visit with you, at least every year.

"Have you asked him to come visit?"

"Yes," I have.

There's a lot of cars on the road today, that's because it's such a nice day.

"Doesn't it feel good to get out?"

"Yes."

They stopped at a red light, and several kids with their parents crossed the street. Soon they got to the highway and were on their way.

A car sped past them; I can't believe that guy went past us like that, a highway is all about going fast.

I can tell that you're probably a more cautious driver than I am. If you want to eat just let me know, we can always go to somewhere get something to eat.

"How old are you now?"

"I'm sixty-nine years old."

Hold on we're going to take a short turn to the right here. I always get gas at this gas station on the right, it always has the best price for gas.

There was a mini golf place that just closed down, I never seen many people there.

You seem to know this area well, that's because I drive through this town to work every day.

My first job was being a waiter at the seafood delight restaurant when I turned eighteen. They drove past a rundown barn, and there were horses in the corral.

They drove down a narrow road and came to the house. This place is out in the country, that's the way he likes it.

They got out of the truck and went over to the front door and knocked on it.

A tall man immediately came to the door. Hello Mike, I have my neighbor Jim with me.

He's been looking for a puppy, go ahead and come in. I'm sorry about how it looks in here, I've been remodeling.

Just follow me I'll show you where the puppies are, the puppies are well taken care of by my wife.

She's not here right now, she's currently at work. There are four male puppies and two females, they're five months old.

Jim sat down on the floor beside them, the puppies were happily playing amongst themselves.

Two of them were cuddling up to Jim's leg, these puppies are very well behaved.

Don't be shy you can pick them up and hold them. He picked up one of the puppies, and it was wagging its tail.

"What's this pups name?"

"Troy"

"Is this puppy available?"

"Yes," he is.

All of the puppies have had their shots and are healthy.

"How much?"

"$500"

He reached in his pocket and took out his wallet and went through his cash and took out $500 and handed it to the man.

He's all yours now, you can rename him if you want. I could tell by your facial expressions that you didn't like his name, you're right.

While he was holding the puppy it licked him on the cheek, this put a smile on his face.

You're such a good puppy, you're so cute. The mother dog came over and sniffed him, then walked back to her puppies and cuddled back in with them. The man handed him a small bag of dog food; you don't have to do that.

I have plenty of food, it's alright. Thanks for everything, you're welcome Sir. Eventually they exited the house and got back into the truck, headed back home.

Your friend Mike is a very polite man but is a man of few words. That's because he just met you for the first time, he's normally like that.

"Do you need anything from the grocery store?"

"No," thanks.

You answered that awfully fast, there's gotta be something that you need. I need some milk for my cereal, and a box of crackers.

That doesn't sound like very much to me, it's just me and I don't eat that much.

Once you're back home I'll go to the grocery store, if there's anything else just tell me. There's a lot of shinny buttons and controls in this vehicle, my truck doesn't have all this in it.

Mine is a 2010 pickup truck, then it's about time you start thinking about getting a new truck. There's nothing wrong with my truck it's just fine for me.

Sometime later he got home, your dog is going to need a leash. I'll get that soon enough; I'm not worried about it right now.

From that day forward Jim and Lewy enjoyed their days together, they laughed and even cried together.

Jim would have his ice cream, while Lewy had biscuits. After dinner leftovers would go to Lewy, then he would jump for joy. While Jim watched television at night, Lewy kept him company.

Jim was feeling like his old self again and would get jittery when his favorite song came on the radio.

Lewy and Jim were good dance partners, and sometimes while Jim sat outback while Lewy would chase after the occasional squirrel.

Often times he would hold Lewy while rocking in his rocking chair and sing to him. This went on for years, Jim remained happy for the rest of his life.

A Day at the Park

It was midafternoon, it was a balmy
eighty degrees, there was a slight breeze
going, and there wasn't even a cloud in
the sky.

It seemed to be a calm day at the park until an older adult showed up with his Chihuahua; his dog would bark at everything and anything; in the nearby tree.

There were two little songbirds perched on a long hanging branch singing happily.

The dog ran over and chased the birds away; they flew high in the sky and were never seen again. Some yards away from the park was a large cornfield; there were some trails that led through the cornfield, the farmer was starting up his tractor.

The elderly man lost control of the leash, and his dog ran across the park and ran over to the farmer.

The farmer yelled out and said get this dog out of here, or you'll be sorry. The older man was a slow walker, it took him just about twenty or minutes to get to where the farmer and his dog were.

The farmer asked is this your dog. He said, yes, this is my dog, I would take full responsibility for it if it bit you, no Sir. It didn't bite me, but I don't like it when dogs I don't know are running around loose.

Call me John, it's nice to meet you John and what's your name, Sir?" "My name is Lenny."

They both shook hands, and Lenny looked down at his dog and said. You bad boy Roger, I thought I taught you better than that.

It's alright, just don't let your dog get loose again, or I'll call the authorities and have you permanently taken off this property.

I won't let it happen again, have a good rest of the day. Lenny bent down and picked up Rodger and walked off towards his Oldsmobile.

Lenny was feeling tired today and quickly got out of his breath; today wasn't a very good day for Lenny; as he walked along, he didn't see a small stick in his way. He almost tripped over it, he regained his balance and continued walking.

He heard a loud sound and Rodger began to bark, as he looked up in the sky and saw a biplane flying low. It was all red, and two people were sitting in it.

It seemed to be flying too low to the ground, the pilot had to be careful not to crash into the trees. It seemed like the pilot was enjoying the scenery, and that's why he was flying the plane so low to the ground.

Lenny looked back down in front of him, and when he did. He saw another person quickly approaching him.

This person had a massive, big-boned German Shepard. This dog looked at his dog and began to lick its chops at Rodger, and Rodger let out a little bark and kept on staring at the other dog.

This dog didn't appreciate this and pulled so hard on the lease that it almost got away from its owner. The owner said, you

bad dog, stop pulling so hard on the leash.
The dog's name was thunder.

Lenny was glad that Thunder hadn't got
away from the owner, or he would have
had a severe problem.

Lenny was beginning to get more out of
breath, so he hurried up some more. He
was only a few feet away from his car.

He opened the driver's side door and sat
down and put Rodger on the passenger
seat. Rodger looked over at Lenny and
began to bark.

What's the matter, you silly dog? After he
said that, Rodger stopped barking and
seemed to have calmed down.

Lenny quickly opened the middle console
and pulled out his inhaler. He took off the

cap, gave himself two puffs of medicine, leaned back in the seat, and gave out a big sigh.

His knee felt like it was cramping up, so he reached down and began to rub it.

After a few minutes of rubbing it, it felt better. He accidentally dropped his inhaler, it fell under his right foot; as he went to bend down, his sunglasses fell off of his face and also dropped down on the floor in front of him.

He picked up both things and began to shake his head. He said to himself, I'm getting so old, and I get out of breath easily.

He thought, maybe I should report the shortness of breath that I get to the Drs.

He closed the driver's side door and
turned on the air conditioner.

However, it wasn't functioning very well.
The car was still so hot inside, Lenny had
an itch on the back of his head and began
to scratch it and looked over at his dog
again.

He put the window down a little bit for
Rodger and put the car in drive and slowly
began to pull out and left the park.

He happened to remember that on this
day he had to go pick up his prescription
at the drug store.

He drove the speed limit the whole time
over to the drug store. All of a sudden
Rodger jumped into the back seat.

Lenny thought oh it won't hurt anything with Rodger being on the back seat.

As he was driving along he saw a car that was swerving all over the road. This driver came up behind him and kept on going all over the road, Lenny was narrowly able to get out of the way. He just pulled over off of the side of the road.

He stayed there until the driver drove past him and then went on his way again to the drug store. After fifteen minutes he had arrived in the parking lot of drug store.

He turned off the air conditioner and said to Rodger I'll be right back. Lenny leaned over and picked up his cane and got out of his car, and slowly began to walk towards the drug store.

There were a lot of people coming and going from the shop next door to the drug store. He saw two little boys walking along with their mother and father and this made him smile.

His head was getting hot from the hot sun beading down on it. He increased his pace and was now entering the drug store.

Each isle in the store was full of people shopping, he walked to the back of the drug store. The guy behind the counter asked him if he was picking up his prescription and in a low voice he said Yes, I am.

He said OKAY! then it's going to cost you a ten-dollar copay, is that alright Sir? Yes, that's okay and he slowly reached back into his pocket.

He pulled out his wallet and looked through it and took out ten dollars. He carefully handed it to the gentleman behind the counter.

He said thank you and gave him the bag with his prescription in it. He walked out of the drug store and all of a sudden felt lightheaded but kept on walking anyway.

It didn't take him long to get back to his car, once back in his car he put down the prescription bag in the middle console.

He pushed in the knob on the radio and the radio came on, it was set to a Christian radio channel. Lenny was very religious and loved listening to Christian music.

Rodger was sleeping in the back seat and was snoring. The hot sun must have tired him out and Rodger fell asleep.

Lenny didn't turn up the radio volume too loud, he just kept it quiet so that it wouldn't wake Rodger.

He pulled out of the parking lot and got out on the main road and was now on his way back home.

Along the way, he accidentally hit a bad bump in the road. It caused Rodger to fall off of the back seat and onto the floor.

He immediately woke up and barked a few times and got resettled on top of the seat.

It took forty-five minutes for Lenny to get back home once he pulled into his driveway. He turned off the radio and put the windows back up and grabbed his prescription.

He said come on Rodgers lets go. Rodger followed him to the front door and walked into his living room.

Lenny lived alone and was married once about twenty years ago but got divorced soon afterwards. He wears a silver necklace.

Lenny went and sat down on the couch, and so did Rodger. He took out the television remote and turned on the television to his favorite religious channel.

Soon afterwards he fell asleep once back in his car he put down the prescription bag in the middle console.

He pushed in the knob on the radio and the radio came on, it was set to a Christian radio channel.

Lenny was very religious and loved listening to Christian music. Rodger was sleeping in the back seat and was snoring; the hot sun must have tired him out and Rodger fell asleep.

A Day in Croppington

There was a small town called

Croppington, which is in Michigan. The

town has a population of just a thousand.

Most of the people in town belong to large

families.

There was a famous family that lived in

this town, their name were the Sabers.

This family knew a lot about growing

crops, they like to grow all their own

vegetables.

The family is vegetarian, this story takes

place a year before World War One began.

The streets of Croppington were always

busy, there was always someone walking up and down the street.

The street was made of cobble stone, sometimes the street would flood from rainstorms. There would sometimes be a lot of mud in the street.

So, to try and get rid of the mud in the street the towns people would put hay down.

Croppington was a very safe place to be, because to get into town you would have to go through a huge gate that was always guarded.

Croppington was a town with a lot of secrets, it's been said that there's a lot of gold under the town.

The gate was very high; in fact, it was seven foot tall. The town of Croppington did come under attack a few years ago.

There were pirates who wanted to destroy the whole town and begin digging for gold.

There were six pirates, and they came from another town. All of the Pirates lost their lives, the guard's towers are eight feet tall.

They are so tall so that the guards can see over the gate, the gate is reinforced by steel. The gate has a large lock on it.

Although the guards don't like to keep the lock on the gate, there are three guardsmen.

All three of the guardsmen wear body armor to protect them from intruders. The three guardsmen had weapons.

There weapons were sniper rifles, and their side arm was a pistol. They would carry extra ammunition just in case.

In the three guards tower, there were fine wooden chairs. The guards would sit down on when they would take a rest, the guard's towers were all winterized and each tower has a window in every direction.

The windows were bullet proof and wouldn't shatter, the towns people don't like the gate or the guard's towers. They just want to get rid of the gate and guard's towers.

Mr. Wobblewort is the mayor of the town.
He's tall, he's about five feet eight. He
wears a cowboy hat and blue jeans; he
has baby blue eyes; they are very
sensitive to light. He wears sunglasses and
known to be stubborn. He doesn't like
bugs; they drive him out of his mind.

One time there was a termite infestation
in his office, he didn't want to return to his
office for a week.

He was sitting in his office when a termite
climbed up his leg and he got so upset
that he almost put himself into a panic
attack.

He ran around the room and almost
ripped his pants off, just because of one
bug.

But he eventually settled down and everything went back to normal. Lewis was a loner; he was the supervisor of the guardsmen.

Every day he would make sure that the guardsmen were up in their towers keeping guard. One of the guardsmen in particular was a stubborn man.

He would back talk some of his friends, so people would no longer talk to him. In town, there was a small knitting mill. Mrs. Swanson and Mrs.

Carrie worked there together. Mrs Swanson was a very demanding woman, who liked things done her way. Mrs Carrie on the other hand was quiet and kept to herself.

Every so often they would talk to each other about how their day was going and so forth.

Just some small talk, every day they would have to be at the knitting mill by eight o clock in the morning.

They both would work till five that evening, Mrs Swanson would always be complaining about little petty things.

One time she told Mrs. Carrie that she wasn't doing her job correctly. Mrs. Carrie asked what do you mean?

I've been working here ever since I was a young girl and I've always done good by my boss.

Alright Carrie I'm sorry I said that to you. I can't accept your apology right now Mrs.

Swanson. Okay Mrs Carrie I'll remember that. The town also had an armory. Mr. Smith worked at the armory.

He enjoyed his job and was always saying to his boss how glad he was to have a good job.

His boss Mr. Dickson was a very controlling man. He would easily lose his temper, when he lost his temper he would be a real bear to work with.

Mr. Dickson would like to smoke a cigar every other day, the smoke would linger on sometimes.

Mr. Smith would never upset his boss because he knew the consequences if he did.

Mr. Smith was an over achiever; he would do more than what he had to do for Mr. Dickson.

Mr. Dickson was an elderly gentleman; he was in his early sixties. He would walk with a slight limp in his left leg, he had a pocket watch in his pocket.

He was bald headed and had some wrinkles on his face. He was hard of hearing and would say could you speak into my good ear? Mr. Smith would have to repeat himself once or twice to Mr. Dickson.

He didn't mind this. Mr. Dickson used to be in the army, he was a lieutenant in the army. On the out skirts of the town was a junkyard.

The junkyard was filled to capacity, the junkyard wasn't too big. It was less than an acre in size.

The walls of the junk yard weren't very tall, sometimes wild animals would wonder into the junkyard.

One time a bear got into junkyard and tried to eat an old tire; the walls of the junkyard were just five feet tall.

There was a small gate that led into the junkyard, everything in the junkyard was free for the taking. In the middle of town was an old water tower.

This water tower has been in town ever since the eighteen hundreds, the water tower was in good shape and was well maintained.

The three legs of the water tower were made of metal and so was the rest of the water tower.

There was some rust on the one leg of the water tower, but it wasn't so bad. The water tower was able to hold two hundred gallons of water.

The water that was in the water tower was from the local river. The local river was a fast-moving river, it had white water Rapids every so often.

There were many sharp rocks in the middle of the river, it was treacherous to cross the river.

In town there was a candy shop, the children were always huddled around the candy shops window.

Their eyes would be wide open, they would stare at the candy man. The candy man's name was Mr. Brown.

He was a tall black man who would walk with a cane, he had a low voice and liked to sing. You could hear him singing his favorite song, amazing grace.

He would sing this song over and over again, he never got bored of singing this particular song, he used to love the holiday season.

He was always so cheerful and always had a smile on his face. During the Christmas season, he would love to sing the song jingle bells.

The children would love to hear Mr. Brown sing Rodolph the red nosed rain deer during Christmas time. Mr. Brown had passed away just recently.

About a year ago, he was working at the candy shop, and he told his boss that he was not feeling so good.

His heart felt like it was pounding, just a few minutes after he said that he fell to the floor and had a heart attack.

His eyes rolled back in his head, he stopped breathing. His boss Steve called a medical team and by the time, they had arrived there was nothing they could have done for him.

His heart stopped and they couldn't revive him, the next day Steve had to tell the towns people the bad news.

The children cried and said we want Mr. Brown back. Steve said I'm sorry I've done all I can do for him, but he has passed away.

The parents to the children said it'll be okay, that day Steve was feeling like being extra nice.

He gave all the kids a free piece of chocolate, the kids were so happy that day. The chocolate gave them so much energy, that the kids kept running around and yelling no more candy man.

At the far end of town was a large area plowed flat land. This is where the town grew its crops, the town was growing six kinds of crops.

These crops include soybeans, corn, potatoes, lettuce, tomatoes, and cabbage. All these crops were in kind of like a green house.

They were well protected from the animals that may wander around the green house like deer or even elk. The crops were in an area that was on four acres.

Their ground had good soil and everything that was planted in it would grow well. There were four people that there only job was to plant and make sure the crops are doing good.

Each day they would water the crops, the crops were always looking good and were always growing better than expected.

The crops would help to feed the whole town, this may be hard to believe but it's how it was.

Around the green house was tall grass, the grass was green and was four foot tall. The plants were planted a few feet away from each other.

This gave the plants enough room to spread out and properly grow, there was an herbalist who worked with the crop growers. The herbalists name was Gary.

Gary was a smart man, he had many skills and loved to work with plants. He would make tonics that he would spray on the plants.

The tonics would help to give the plants a quick growth spurt, he would rap the seeds in a custom package and plant them while they were in the packages.

There was only one time when the crops in town weren't growing so well, that's when Gary the herbalist was hired. Gary was a middle-aged man; he was in his late thirties.

He had good vision and didn't need to wear glasses, he had short hair, he didn't like to have long hair; he would go to the Barbers and have his hair cut.

He had green eyes and always dressed nice; he always likes to wear his black leather vest; the vest was made out of bull hide.

There were six buttons on the vest, he always kept the sixth button undone. He didn't like to be in tight spaces for long.

That's one of his phobias, every day he works on getting over his fears. One time he tried to go to the local hypnotist.

To see if he could get over his fears. But sadly, it didn't work the way he wanted it to. He has two sisters and an older brother.

He gets along well with his large family. However, him and his brother don't get along very well.

They're always arguing about something. Gary doesn't always like to talk with his brother. Gary went to college for a course called experimental bio engineering. He took the class for four years.

He has been given an award for creating seeds that can grow into a plant in just a week. Gary is so glad to have received this achievement.

He would always study for tests and was an A student, he would always stride for good grades. While the other students would have parties on the weekend, Gary would stay home and study.

While he was in the class he took forty tests, each week he would have to take a test. The tests were always given out on a Friday.

The other students would go off and party afterwards, Gary took a test one time and got a B on it.

He was so upset about getting a B that he took the test over again and was able to get an A on it.

He jumped for joy that Friday afternoon. He was a neat freak, he liked to keep his papers filed and put away neatly. Gary had a puppy; his name was Paps.

Paps always had a lot of energy; he liked to jump around and would lick your face if you let him.

Gary taught Paps a few tricks, like Paps would jump up into the air and do a back flip and land on his four feet.

Gary would study for a few hours and then he would take Paps to the local park. The local park was a stretch of land that was just two acres.

The land had green grass growing all around, the ground was even and a nice area to have a small park. Other people would bring their dogs there too.

Gary doesn't like to sit still; he always has to be doing something. He had one hobby that he enjoyed doing.

He like to whittle wood into birds, he has made three bird sculptures out of pine wood.

He keeps his sculptures on the shelf above the fireplace, he had four wooden bird sculptures on the shelf but one of them fell down into the fireplace and was burned and was ruined.

Gary has a rare condition that causes his legs to swell up every so often. He's an herbalist, he came with his own medicine to combat his health problem.

He made a tonic of medicine that he drinks each morning with his breakfast, he isn't much of a breakfast eater.

Somedays he skips breakfast and then it makes him feel bad and have no energy. He doesn't sleep a whole lot; he can get by on just a few hours of sleep.

He sleeps on a cot and doesn't like to sleep without his favorite pillow and blanket.

The blanket is made out of wool and keeps him nice and warm in the winter months. It wasn't wintertime yet; the blanket was black and red.

Gary wouldn't use this blanket every night though, he used a lighter blanket for the summertime and the heavier wool blanket for the wintertime. Gary liked the wintertime.

He likes the snow and the blizzards; he has a thick winter coat that he wears out in blizzards.

It keeps him warm even in the worst blizzards, the worst blizzard was when there was five inches of snow on the ground. But Gary didn't mind this.

He just stayed in house until the bad

blizzard was over, the blizzard only lasted

a few hours and then was over.

The snow piled up all around Gary's house

and he wasn't able to open his front or

back door. This sure was frustrating to

him.

For he didn't like having to be stuck inside

for more than a few hours. Even in the

wintertime they would grow crops in the

green house.

They would never stop growing plants, the

plants were what fed the town. Gary's

mom Sara is always worrying about him,

she was sad to see him go off to college.

Gary always tells her not to worry about

him and that he's fine.

"Why do you always have to think that you're fine and not want you to worry about me?"

"It's just how I am, and I'm not going to change now."

That's no way to be, I know but I've been really busy lately and haven't had any time to relax. I'm feeling a little grumpy because I didn't sleep well for the past week.

I have to catch up on my sleep. I'll eventually calm down and not be so grumpy.

I feel bad when I get grumpy with you mom, but sometimes it happens. That night Gary couldn't sleep, he kept on tossing and turning, at one point he threw the blankets off of his bed and let out a yawn. For some reason, he couldn't stop thinking about his job. Then he slowly fell into a deep sleep and went into a dream. He dreamt about a ghost that lived in his town.

He had never had such a strange dream, he kept on dreaming and in his dream the ghost was telling him that he should leave the town Croppington, because bad things were going to happen.

He has lived in the town all of his life and now a ghost in his dream is telling him he should leave. He tried to wake up but couldn't seem to open his eyes.

He was so comfortable in bed that he had no reason to move or get up. Then the ghost in his dream said that there was going to be a surprise attack on Croppington in the next day or so. He quickly woke up and walked around his room thinking about what the ghost had just told him in the dream.

He began to pack up his stuff into his travel case and quickly threw a few shirts and pants into his large suitcase.

Then he pulled out his cell phone and dialed his mother's phone number, it kept ringing and there was no answer.

He left a message, he said I don't know if this is true or not, but I was told the town was going to be attacked tomorrow.

I love you and have a good rest of the day. He quickly opened the front door and ran out of his house, we waved down a taxi and the taxi quickly pulled over and let him in. The taxi driver was an old man with a long gray beard.

"Where would you like to go?"

"I would like to go to the airport, okay that'll cost you fifty dollars."

"Why are you in such a rush if you don't mind me asking?"

"I heard that this town was going to be attacked tomorrow."

I've never heard of something so dumb in my life, this town is the safest town in the United States.

You have your reasons for thinking that this town could be attacked, I've never thought that this town would be attacked again.

It took forty-five minutes to get to the airport, once there he checked in his luggage and looked for the flight that was going to Houston Texas.

The terminal for the flight to Houston was all the way on the other side of the airport.

He ran over there, he got out of breath. But found a chair and sat down and was able to sit down for a while.

He looked down at his cell phone and was hoping that his mother was going to call him.

He had his passport and driver's license with him tucked away in his back pocket.

The flight was going to leave in one hour from Croppington, Gary was relieved that the plane was going to take off so soon. Then an hour quickly passed, it was now time to board the plane, there weren't too many people on this flight though.

Within a matter of minutes everyone was boarded and settled in. Then the plane took off and Gary put his head back in his seat and took a short nap before he knew it they were landing in Houston Texas.

Once he got off of the plane he found his luggage and walked to the nearby hotel, the rest of his day went so fast, he looked down at wristwatch and it was already four in the afternoon.

He went to the nearby restaurant and got a chicken sandwich and returned back to his hotel room.

He was tired and fell asleep rather quickly in the bed, the next morning he got a call from his mother.

She said the governors house was blown up and the front gate of the town was blown down, were being forced to leave the town, so what you said was right I should have listened to you.

"Are you all right?"

"Yes," I'm fine, I'll talk to you later.

I love you bye, in the weeks following the incident the town was cleaned up and everything went back to normal.

Falcon Trail

In 2028 there was an off-road truck competition. There were three classes of trucks that were allowed to enter the race.

First you had the prostock class, then the second class was the custom class. The Final class of truck is the full custom class.

These trucks had huge amounts of horsepower; this race took place in Peru. There were only a few different tracks that they could race on.

Each track was different in size and shape. However, one of the tracks would pass right by a large, beautiful waterfall.

Although the driver's don't have the time
to look at the beautiful waterfalls, through
the years there have been many crashes.

There was just one fatal crash, the driver
of the truck slammed on the brakes and
wasn't quick enough and crashed off a
cliff.

He fell eighty feet to his death; his truck
had fallen into pieces. Ever since the crash
the owners of the track have put up a
large guard rail.

The trucks had special designed tires that
were made for dirt, the tires would give
the trucks better handling and good
traction control.

The dirt tracks would go on for miles and seemed like they would go on forever, although in reality they were not too long. It would take the drivers four hours to complete the track and go across the finish line.

There was one driver in particular who had won the one race twice, people say that he wins the races because he has good luck on his side.

He always tells everyone that it's not luck that helps him to win, and that's it's just because he is so skilled at what he does.

His name is Timmy, his copilots name is Jimmy. They have raced alongside each other for many years.

Timmy shares his winnings with Jimmy, he gives him a fifty-fifty split of all the money that he makes.

Timmy has won five racing campaign ship races; he doesn't get upset if he loses a race. He just says to Jimmy better luck next time.

When they aren't racing they're on vacation in Argentina, Timmy has a nice luxurious house in Argentina. He has been married for five years and his marriage has remained strong over the years.

He just turned twenty-eight years old, and his wife Mary is two years younger than he is, but it doesn't bother him.

For the both of them it was love at first sight and they have remained deeply in love and nothing every comes between them.

They had a big wedding with their entire family and some close friends. His mom bought him a special cake that had a picture of his wife and him on the cake. He thanked his mom and told her much the cake had ment to him.

Timmy is a very thoughtful man, that gets along well with anyone. He never has had an attitude towards his wife Mary and they both live their lives the same.

They're perfect for each other, and they hope to stay married til the end of time. He got married in July, he had a special firework show done over his house.

The fireworks were very expensive and cost a few thousand dollars, although he did not care how much they cost.

As of lately him and his wife have been thinking about having a son or daughter, however they would both prefer if it was a boy.

They already have the crib set up and ready for a baby, a few of his friends have had kids and say that their kids are just wonderful and brighten up their days each and every day. Timmy's last name is Cod, but he does not like his last name, it says it's not a good last name because it's too short. Timmy's parents had three kids including him.

Two out of the three of them were boys and there was one girl. Timmy's parents would have a lot of disagreements they didn't split up, but we're thinking about it.

His parents are very old fashion and refuse to learn about computers or anything that deals directly with technology.

Over the years Timmy has tried to get them interested more in computers, but they just ignore him when he goes to teach them a simple computer lesson.

His parents do own a desktop computer, but they don't use it very often if at all. It must have two layers of dust on it by now and has been sitting on their home desk for more than three years and hasn't been turned on for more than a year.

Neither one of his parents own a cell phone, they say we don't need a cell phone it's just another expensive gadget we will have to pay for.

Timmy tells them that they should have a cell phone in case of an emergency, and they give him a dirty look.

His dad is more stubborn then his mom is. One time his mom argued with his dad over the television bill. Neither one of them like to watch much television.

They would rather spend their days outside gardening the beautiful garden, in their garden there are annual plants that come up every year.

His moms favorite flower is the rose, and for her seventy first birthday he got her a rose bush, which she immediately planted the next day.

Her favorite kind of fruit is pears, she says that she likes how sweet they taste and each day she eats two pears, but his dad Paul thinks that she is eating too much fruit each day and that she might get sick from eating all of the fruit.

A few months ago, she ate a bad pear and it caused her to throw up for an hour or two, but it didn't stop her from continuing to eat the pears.

She says the sweeter the pear the better, and one time she made a pear pie, but Paul didn't like it and threw it away when she wasn't looking.

She couldn't believe that he did that and still to this day can't forgive him for throwing her pie away.

She said to him why don't you ask me before you do something like that. Paul always says I'm sorry, and she always says well sorry doesn't get my pie back.

Then she went on to say you realize that it took me an hour to bake that pie and I paid good money for those three pears that I used in the pie. I have heard about enough.

Now were going to talk about a different topic, Timmy always makes sure that he takes a day out of the week and goes over and visits his mother and father. They're up in age, they live alone. This sometimes causes Timmy to get worried about them.

He stays over at their house for an hour or two and watches television with them. They both have been retired for fifty years.

Nancy used to work in a knitting mill making fine sweatshirts. While Paul was a heavy machinery operator, he would drive a D10 dozer. When he first started with the construction company, they had him driving a forklift.

He didn't like to drive the forklift because he was nervous that the forklift would drop the load. He would carefully drive the forklift, and one time he almost tipped over the forklift because he put too many bags of concrete on the front of the forklift. The forklift could easily handle five bags of concrete, but he added more to it.

He had each bag of concrete piled up
nicely, one of the bags almost slipped and
fell. He was quick enough to catch the bag
of concrete.

It was easy to control the forklift, there
were two handles that would make the
forklift go into gear and a large black
steering wheel and the whole thing was
green and the front of it was white.

It wasn't the most powerful of the forklift
models, its tires were no larger than that
of a lawn mower. It could only go a slow
five miles per hour, it would take Paul an
hour to finish his job each day.

He was always a very hard worker; he
wasn't afraid of the snow and ice and
would come to work when no one else
could.

He would drive a 1984 Four-wheel drive
pickup truck. He had put on it a few
Harley Davidson decals, and the decals
looked good on his all-black truck.

The truck had a custom exhaust and
would sound nice and loud when he drove
down the street. He bought the truck with
cash, he doesn't always like to pay with
his debit card.

From operating the D10 dozer he had
developed back issues from always being
bounced around in the dozer. He says that
it was always a childhood dream of his to
drive a dozer, but now since his back got
hurt. He doesn't want to drive or even
look at another dozer again. He said I've
done my long years of hard work, now
since I'm retired I can rest my old aching

back. For a while he was seeing the Dr

every month for his bad lower back pain.

He tried to go to a chiropractor every

other day, but that didn't relieve his pain.

He had to take a pain pill for his back pain

every day.

He would have to take one pill in the

morning and one pill in the evening before

he would fall asleep at night.

He was never a complainer, after a while

the pain would get to him, and it would

make him grumpy.

His boss would always have him very busy

and was a slave driver, he wouldn't quit

until the whole job was done. However, he

had a big ego and would often cuss at

Paul, he didn't appreciate getting yelled at.

He would try to belittle his workers and some of the workers put him on notice that if he didn't stop treating them like that, that they were going to quit.

After a day or so he changed his attitude towards his workers, everything went back to normal.

Some of the workers were living paycheck to paycheck and didn't even have enough money to afford health insurance.

Timmy has to have good health insurance because of his racing career, at one point in his life he didn't have health insurance and now he can't live without being on health insurance. He pays a few hundred dollars each month for his health insurance. Timmy is very generous and likes to give his extra money away to charities.

He likes to give his money to the charity that helps the mentally ill patients pay for their medicines. The number on his truck is nine, which is his favorite number.

He says it's his lucky number nine and the number nine is in big bold letters on the top and side of his trophy truck.

He spends a lot of extra money on his truck to make sure it stays in good shape. He is always having to buy new suspension, for it because he hits some big bumps, it throws the truck all around.

He knows that someday if he's not careful
he is going to have a bad back just like his
father. Timmy is a good driver, but he
cannot avoid every big bump on the track.

When he gets in his truck he has to climb
in through the window, he's in good shape
and doesn't mind climbing in and out of
the trophy truck.

He's always tuning the motor every
chance that he gets. His truck is all four-
wheel drive and has independent
suspension.

Timmy is hoping that someday when he
retires from racing, he will be able to have
a more relaxed lifestyle.

He wants to have a son and a daughter
someday. He is always thinking about his

little nephew Caleb, he's five years old.
Timmy likes to hold Caleb and his parents
bring him over to visit. He just visits twice
a month, he's always busy in between
visits.

Timmy signed himself up for the campaign
ship race and said to himself I want this to
be the second to last race that I ever do.

A week went by, he raced in the
campaign-ship race that was held in Peru.
He went through the checkered flag and
won the race.

He immediately jumped out of his truck
and gave his copilot a hug and said we did
it again.

He was awarded a trophy and a gold medal and to this day he has never forgotten about that day.

He's now almost seventy-five years old and has three kids. Their names were Larry, Sam, Timmy Jr. He lived out the rest of his life with his wife and kids.

Rock a Bye Baby

Ava had a healthy baby when she was twenty-five years old, she named the baby Dwayne Lee Michael. Dwayne was a regular sized baby and liked to suck on his thumb.

Ava had an old rocking chair on the front porch of her house. The rocking chair would lean back just enough to make Ava comfortable.

Right after Ava had her baby she would make sure that she would get plenty of exercise.

She bought Dwayne a nice carriage so that she could walk him around the neighborhood.

Ava knows all her neighbors by a first name basis and likes to strike up conversations with her elderly neighbors.

The house to the left of her house belongs to an elderly woman whose name is Emma.

Emma likes to work on her vegetable garden during the summer months and likes to bake cookies all winter long.

One year Emma came over and gave Ava a whole tin full of Christmas cookies, Ava was so thankful to have such a kind caring neighbor.

Emma's husbands name is Neil, Neil is a professional golfer and retired when he was sixty-five years old.

But he still likes to keep busy and now is a greeter at a store, he doesn't really like his job, but is just glad that he can get out of the house.

Emma doesn't mind being alone for the day, Neil has to get up at nine o clock in the morning and works till two in the afternoon.

It seems like an unusual workday, but just the other day Neil went to the Dr. the Dr. said that his liver wasn't functioning properly and that it would fail soon.

Emma was so upset over the news that she did not want Neil to go to work that day. Emma cried for an hour and talked to Neil about what the Dr. had said.

Neil didn't want to be bothered about it and slammed the front door and walked out on Emma. Emma couldn't believe what kind of person that her husband had turned into. She was immediately saddened and walked into her bedroom and pulled out a book out of her library of books.

Emma mostly liked to read romance novels and would sometimes have dreams after reading the books. Emma has a daughter that no longer lives in the United States.

Her name is Isabella, and she is married to a marine. She has been married to him for going on three years now. His name is Julio, and he treats her very well.

In the next coming month, her daughter is expecting to have twins. Emma is so happy for her daughter; everyday Emma likes to call her daughter and check on her. Emma has been feeling more despair and loneliness and calls her kids more often.

Ava would sit on the rocking chair each night at six o clock and gently rock back and forth until Dwayne would fall asleep.

If Ava wouldn't rock Dwayne, he would cry out and suck on his little fingers. One-time Ava was rocking Dwayne and she fell asleep.

That night there was a bad thunderstorm, and it knocked her hanging plants right off of the hooks that held them up.

One of the hanging plants, came crashing down just a few feet away from her head, and it woke up her up and it caused her to jump up.

She still had a tight grip on Dwayne. Ava nor Dwayne were injured but it shook her up. Once she stood back up, she looked around and it was still raining so hard.

Then all of a sudden, the wind began to blow at ten miles per hour, and the rain began to blow in towards her.

Ava retreated back into the house and felt a cramp, in her lower calf. It hurt so bad, that she had to quickly run up to her bed and sit down on it.

This whole time she was still cradling Dwayne. Dwayne would open his eyes every once in a while and he fell back to sleep. Ava carefully put Dwayne on the bed and let him lie down.

Ava was feeling hungry but didn't want to leave her babies side. Suddenly Dwayne woke up again and began to roll back and forth and was crying at the same time. Ava doesn't like to hear her baby cry, not even a minute. Dwayne had a grin on his face, and Ava said to him, I hope that you can relaxed again.

Ava finally decided to take Dwayne into the kitchen with her, she carefully walked down the one step into her kitchen.

She put Dwayne in one of the kitchen chairs and made sure that he was secure in the chair. She turned her back to Dwayne and began to go through the refrigerator.

She was hungry for an orange but couldn't find one, she was getting irritated because she couldn't find an orange. She pulled out two plastic drawers and began to dig through them. The one drawer was full of broccoli and peas and carrots. Then the drawer next to that, had onions and radishes.

One of the onions was all mushy and had a rank smell to it, she quickly tossed the onion in the trash can that was next to the refrigerator.

Ava turned to look at Dwayne and he was leaning on the table and was fast asleep and began to lean over to his left side and almost fell.

This made Ava very nervous, so she quickly ran over and picked him up and held him. She could still smell the rotten onion. While she was holding the baby she went out to her one car garage and placed the trash can inside the garage and slammed the garage door behind her. This caused Dwayne to shift and almost made him fall, but Ava was quick enough to get a better grip on him, and he settled back down.

Ava was beginning to get hot and sweated, and wiped the sweat off of her forehead, letting out a sigh. You know

Dwayne, you're such a good baby, I'm so glad you're so healthy.

Okay Dwayne mommies s getting tired, so I'm going to go back in my bedroom and take a nap with you.

Ava's neighbor that lived to the right of her was an elderly man whose name was Darren; he used to be a dog trainer and has three dogs of his own.

Ava doesn't like his dogs; his dogs are large and like to bark a lot. One day she was taking out the trash and one of his large Rottweiler got lose from its pen and came running towards Ava.

Luckily saw the dog coming and ran inside and the dog jumped up at her front door.

Ava sat her baby on the bed, it was feeling, extra hot in the bedroom.

Ava quickly walked out of her bedroom and walked out into the kitchen. She opened the side door and walked out upon the concrete slab where the air conditioner compressor was.

The compressor was so loud and looked to be running just fine, she bent over and felt the left side of the compressor. It felt so cold, she couldn't understand why. There was ice formed all around the top of the compressor, Ava hadn't noticed this and now saw it and was aware of it.

She found a small stick on the ground next to the compressor, she took the stick and tried to use it to break the ice off of the compressor.

She wasn't able to even get one piece of ice off of the top of the compressor. This made her frustrated, she kept on trying, eventually from trying to get rid of the ice the little stick broke in half and after that she gave up on it.

She threw the stick down and with anger went back into her house. The house still felt so hot inside and she couldn't stand it.

It was now the middle of the afternoon; the house should haven't been this hot. She was getting more concerned about the house being hot and didn't want her baby to get too hot.

She went upstairs to her room and checked on her baby. Dwayne was sleeping just fine, but she saw that he was sweating. Then decided to wipe off his forehead with a baby wipe.

Dwayne didn't stir when she wiped his forehead off. I'm sorry Dwayne but it's entirely too hot in this house for you.

Mommies going to have to take you somewhere cooler, I hope that's going to be okay with you Dwayne.

Ava thought to herself where I'm going to go to, a thought came into her mind, it was a pleasant thought. She thought to herself I'm going to visit my mom.

She took out the babies blanket and took out his stroller and baby bottle. She threw it all into a small suitcase and picked up and this caused him to wake up, he woke up and let out a loud cry, oh baby it's going to be okay.

I just want to take you to my mom's house for a day, Ava picked up the suitcase with her hand while she held Dwayne.

She carefully walked over to her Mini Cooper and opened the back-left door and placed Dwayne in the car seat. She carefully strapped him in, and he closed his eyes.

Dwayne was feeling at ease and Ava was glad, he threw the suitcase in the back of the car then got In.

It felt so hot inside of the car, so she put on the air conditioning on low and drove down the block.

She was driving the speed limit and it
didn't take her long to reach the highway.

Once on the highway she noticed that
there was so much traffic, she couldn't
stand it. She took out her iPhone and
dialed her mom's cell phone number. It
rang a few times then her mother picked
up.

"Hi who is this?"

"It's your daughter, oh now I know
who you are."

"What's the matter?"

"My central air system has stopped
working, and the house is too hot
for my baby."

"How's your baby doing?"

"He's doing good, and is growing up
so fast, babies do grow up so fast."

"Have you taken him to the
playground lately?"

"Yes"

"Did he enjoy it?"

"No," it was too hot outside for him.

"Do you take Dwayne outside
often?"

"Yes," I do, and he loves it outside.
But these ninety-degree days are
hard on all of us.

"Why didn't you call anyone first
about your air conditioner before
calling me?"

"I wasn't sure who to call, how can you be not sure who to call?"

"You could have easily turned on your laptop and looked up air conditioner repairmen from there and you would have gotten everything fixed up right away."

I wanted to come over anyway, I wish you would have called me earlier.

"Why mom?"

"I have a hairdresser appointment in two hours."

That's okay, we can just go with you to the hairdresser. But that's not fair to you, mom don't worry about me. I didn't know that you stopped washing your hair.

"How long has this been going on?"

"A month ago, I stopped being able to wash my own hair."

My arms are getting weaker, I can barely get my arms over my head. I feel so bad for you.

"Do your arms hurt?"

"Yes," they hurt me tremendously every day, I have to take two Advil just for the pain to go away.

"Have you called Dr Lucas lately and told him about your arm pain?"

"Yes," I have, he said that he's going to set up an appointment for me next week.

Don't let him push you around mom, I won't, I'm worried about you, I think that you need to go to the Drs today.

If you want, I'll take you to the emergency room and let them do all the tests on you.

No, I don't want to go to the emergency room, that's final, now don't ask me again.

"Where are you right now?"

"I'm sitting in a long line of traffic."

There's so much traffic that I'm going to be waiting another thirty minutes until I can get off at my exit.

"Do you want me to have anything ready for you?"

"You don't have to go into all that trouble to make dinner for me."

I'll just go to subway if it gets too late before we get back home. You're my daughter and I want to cook for you, now please.

"Do you like meat loaf?"

"Yes"

"Why?"

"I could make that for you and Wayne."

You can, but let me help you make it, no I can cook it myself. Yeah but your arms are hurting you.

I know but please don't worry I have the Advil container right next to me. Mom that's not funny, it's not funny to joke around about pain.

Calm down everything will be okay. I'm calm mom; it's just I'm worried that you are taking too many Advil.

"Why don't you just take Aleve?"

"No," it doesn't work the same as Advil does.

"How's the traffic?"

"It seems to be moving along."

"How's Dwayne doing in the back seat?"

"He seems to be sleeping for now."

"Have you given him a lollipop lately?"

"No," I haven't, he doesn't need the sugar.

All kids love to eat candy, yes but I don't want Dwayne to have any candy.

"How about the sugarless kind of candy?"

"Do me a favor and drop the subject."

"How long until you get here?"

"I don't know the exact time I'll be there; I would think that within twenty-five minutes I'll be there."

That sounds good to me, I'm making the meatloaf right now and it should be good this time. I remember the last time that you made meat loaf and forgot about it in the oven, it got burned to a crisp.

I'm going to let you know that I'm going to hang up now. I love you mom and I'll see you soon.

Bye now, Ava put her phone back in her pocket and the traffic let up and she got off at her exit.

She drove down a side road, it only took her five minutes to reach her mom's house.

Once in the driveway she took off her seat belt and opened the driver's door and got out. She walked back to the rear of the car and opened the back door.

Dwayne was still fast asleep, she felt bad
having to wake him up. Dwayne opened
his eyes and began to cry out.

It's going to be all right, let mommy hold
you. I don't like it when you cry Dwayne.
Dwayne let out a yawn, his little eyes
went shut once more.

You're being a good baby now; my mom
is going to be delighted to see you and I'm
going to be make sure you stay happy. All
of a sudden, her mom opened the front
door and slowly came walking out.

"How are you doing?"

"I'm doing good"

I'm just getting the baby out of the car
and getting his things together.

"Do you need help carrying

something?"

"Yes," I need help carrying the

suitcase, but mom I don't want you

to overly strain your arms lifting

anything that is more than ten

pounds.

Now you are talking like my Dr, and I

don't appreciate it. Now just drop the

conversation about my arms and we can

proceed.

Awe your baby is so cute, it's so cute how

he sleeps. He looks like you and has blue

eyes just like you.

Come on in don't be shy, I will I just have

to make sure that I have Dwayne tightly

in my arms then I'll be in. Once Ava

walked into the house and she could smell the fragrance of the meat loaf.

The meat loaf smells so good; it didn't take you very long to prepare it. I have my ways about getting things done in a hurry.

"What else did you make along with the meatloaf?"

"I made a green bean casserole, and I have some apple sauce to go along with the meal."

Oh, good Dwayne loves his apple sauce; how did you know he likes Apple sauce? You told me once before. Now I remember that mom.

"How's Lance doing?"

"You mean my ex, yes?" I haven't heard from him in almost a year.

I can't believe that you and he were together for three months and put up with his abusive behavior. I can't believe that he had made you pregnant.

Oh, stop it; you know that I wanted to have a baby. But you should have had a baby with a man who truly loves you.

At that point in my life, I didn't have the best man to live with. You're young yet and haven't learned all the lessons that I've learned.

At least you had a good life, my life has been a struggle and I'm getting tired of it all. Just be thankful that you have a healthy baby, and you are staying healthy.

That's true, now let me get the meatloaf out of the oven and then we can eat.

"Are you going to put Dwayne in the booster chair?"

"Yes," I am, just give me a moment. Ava gently placed Dwayne down in the booster chair, and he opened his beautiful blue eyes.

Ava's mother grabbed her oven mitts and put them on and opened the oven, Ava could feel the heat coming from the oven and it made her sweat. That meatloaf looks great and so does the green bean casserole.

Ava's mother placed everything on the table and now they were ready to chow down.

I can't wait to try your meatloaf. Ava took

a forkful of meatloaf and gave Dwayne

some apple sauce. Wow that meatloaf is

incredible, I love everything that you

make.

Ava and her mom enjoyed their dinner

and so did Dwayne later that evening they

all grew tired and watched some television

and they all fell asleep.

Skittles the Cat

Skittles was an all-white cat with long fur and had long skinny whiskers. He's always full of energy, he likes to be petted and scratched.

Sometimes he'll roll over onto his back and let his owner Harriet rub his belly. He has a sweet tooth though; his favorite kind of sweets are jellybeans.

He has been really lazy lately though, and just sleeps on the couch. He has been trained to use the toilet and isn't very happy about it.

One time he fell into the toilet and didn't feel good for the rest of the day. He had leaped out of the toilet and the toilet bowl water was cold and caused him to shake. Harriet wasn't pleased with his behavior and was about ready to kick him out of her house. Harriet had grabbed a towel from the bathroom to dry him off.

But he wanted nothing to do with her, he ran out of the bathroom and went into the kitchen. Harriet is an older woman who was a ballerina in her younger years.

She just turned seventy-five years old and was still living the American dream, she was never married and there was a good reason for it.

As a young woman, she was always on the move and liked to go back packing in Denali national park in Alaska.

In all her years of backpacking she has visited every state park and is glad she did while she was still young. Now she plans on living out the rest of her years at home and live a quiet life with her cat skittles. She has two nice neighbors that live on either side of her.

Although she only goes outside when she has to, she lives in Arizona now and used to live in Kentucky when she was still living with her parents.

Sadly, though her parents have passed away so time ago. It's been more than fifteen years since they're gone.

Harriet still has many photo albums with her parents in it. Every now and then she'll open the photo album and browse through it looking at all the good times that they used to have together.

Harriet still has three good friends that she graduated with in high school. They're dear friends and come over once a year to see how Harriet is doing.

Her friends love her cat, they say how cute he is. They cuddled up beside him and squeeze him like he's a soft teddy bear.

Although her cat doesn't like to be squeezed, he just lets them do it anyway. Her friends ask Harriet if they could have her cat, her answer is always no it's my cat and I love him very much.

Her friend Grendel comes over every other week and buys Harriet groceries, Harriet thanks her friend for the groceries. Her friend spends so much money on food, almost two hundred dollars of food.

But she doesn't have much cash on her, she uses her four credit cards to pay for the food.

Harriet doesn't like to go out grocery shopping, because she tends to lose track of where she had parked her car. She drives an old Buick la Saber.

She has had this car for five years and it's broke down on her twice in the past two years.

One time she was driving down the bypass and the check engine light lit up on the dashboard.

Then the car began to slow down, and smoke came bellowing out of the hood. She couldn't believe that this was happening to her, she thought I guess I'm going to have a bad day today.

Once her car came to a stop she pulled out her smart phone and went onto Google and looked for a local towing company.

A bunch of names came up on her phone and she wasn't sure who she wanted to call. She closed her eyes and placed her finger on the screen and saw that her finger had landed on Coberts towing and car repair.

She dialed the number and a man answered and said to her my name is France's, and how may I help you Ma'am?"

"My car broke down somewhere on the bypass and I need to be towed."

"How are you going to pay today?"

"I'll pay you with cash."

"Why must you ask me that question?"

Ma'am we deal with so many people and some people haven't paid us for all the work that we did. This is how we make sure that you are going to paying for our services.

"How much is it going to cost Sir?"

“It's going to cost you sixty dollars and ninety-nine cents.”

“What's with the ninety-nine cents?”

“Listen man I don't know it's just how much I charge.”

If you have any more questions about the cost and fees you can talk to my manager.

It seems like you have a problem with me Sir, no I don't have any problem with you.

I just get tired of you asking me so many questions. It's a good thing to ask questions, yes, it is Ma'am, but were always so swamped with work and don't have the time to answer hundreds of questions that you may ask.

All right that's enough, okay so what's your name? My name is Harriet, how comes you didn't ask me for my name straight away.

I don't know, I'm not going to continue on arguing with you over petty nonsense.

"How long until you can send someone out?"

"I'm notifying my main mechanic now, so that means he'll be out within the hour. But I have to be at my hairdressers in three hours."

"Do you think I'll be able to make my appointment?"

"You should have plenty of time to get there in time."

All right I'm going to let you go now and call me back if he doesn't show up. Okay bye now.

She hung up the phone and placed it back in her purse. She has a designer pocketbook and has a lot of bling on it.

The purse itself is made out of leather and has a bunch of beads on it. She likes shiny things with a lot of bling. She put her car in park and just sat there waiting for the tow truck driver.

The inside of the car was getting warm, so she cranked up the air conditioning and leaned her head back into the soft comfortable seat. She felt her self-falling asleep, but kept her eyes open any way.

The cars and trucks were zooming past
her, and they weren't doing the speed
limit.

A tractor trailer driving way to fast went
by her and one of the tires on the tractor
trailer blew out.

The tractor trailer lost control and crashed
into three cars and one truck that was
ahead of her.

Harriet thought to herself oh great now I
have witnessed a severe accident.

The tractor trailer flipped onto its side and
the cars that he ran into remained
motionless.

Twenty minutes later two Police cruisers
showed up and so did an ambulance.

Harriet couldn't believe that the tow truck driver didn't show up.

She was about to call back the towing company and complain, but she saw a large flatbed truck pull up to her car.

The driver of the flatbed truck wasn't too happy, he had the look of disgust on his face. He had a long black handlebar mustache and was wearing a baseball cap.

He looked Harriet and put the window down and asked your Harriet, right?"

"Yes"

"What's your name?"

"My name is Mario, and you're not the only one who needs a tow today."

I was just called and told them that I'll have to tow away three more vehicles. Oh, my goodness you have a lot of work, yes, I do.

You're going to have to bear with me while I tow the other cars then your car. Wait a moment, I want you to tow my car first. Pay me a hundred dollars and I'll tow your car right now.

Wait I wasn't told that it was going to cost an additional one hundred dollars. Listen, I don't have the time to argue with you.

Now do you want to give me the hundred dollars so I can get started on towing your car. You make it sound like such a hassle to tow my car, what's it going to take you five minutes to get the car on the lift.

Look Harriet you have no idea what it takes to tow a car, you have a bad attitude.

"Where's the money?"

"Hold on I have to open my pocketbook to get to my wallet so that I can get to the money. Here's the hundred dollars, all right Ma'am I'm now going to work on it."

It will take me a half an hour to get your car loaded up.

"Is that going to be okay?"

"That'll be fine, I'll just wait longer. Harriet crossed her arms and was feeling irritated. She was so irritated that she couldn't sit still no longer."

She was thinking about laying her head back but decided that she was going to get out of her car but didn't realize what was going to happen next.

Meanwhile at her house Skittles was having a good time, he was running up and down the steps that led up to the bedroom.

Inside of the toy that he was playing with, there was cat nip. He wanted nothing more than to get to the cat nip.

He pounced on the toy repeatedly and let out his sharp claws and scratched the toy all up.

The toy was not in the best shape and began to fall apart, first some string was hanging off of it. Then it came further apart and was not in two halves.

The cat nip went all over the carpeting and skittles wasn't watching where he was going and walked into a tall vase knocking it over on the hardwood floor in the kitchen. The vase had artificial flowers it and some of the artificial flowers fell out onto the floor. Then he began to pat around the artificial flowers making even more of a mess.

He looked up at the counter and saw the cat dish, he immediately jumped up on the main counter in the kitchen and was looking in the candy dish.

The candy dish was full of different colored jellybeans. The jellybeans smelled so good to him that he put his paw in the dish and took out some jellybeans, he quickly scarfed them up and licked his chops afterwards.

He enjoyed them so much that he almost forgot to chew them up and one whole jellybean went down his throat. He coughed and the jellybean went straight down to his stomach.

His stomach began to grumble, he let out a big burp. He looked out the window and a bird was looking in at him.

He licked his chops again but this time at the bird. He took a moment to eat the rest of the jellybeans, he must of ate thirty jellybeans.

He licked his chops and then laid down for a moment. The bird landed on the windowsill almost like it was tempting the cat.

He thought about leaping over to the windowsill to check out the bird closer. He leaped over and was now by the windowsill and the little bird flew away and made him feel like he leaped over there for nothing.

He decided to leap back down on the floor and took a stroll into the living room. The large fish tank that was in the living room, had many beautiful fish in it.

Skittles sat back and watched the fish swim back and forth for a while and tried to stand up on his back legs and paw at the side of the fish tank.

The glass didn't crack or anything, but he continued on pawing at the glass, and it began to crack.

Although it was just a slight crack, and no water came out. But he hit the fish tank so hard the next time that the glass shattered, and the fifty-gallon aquarium spilled out all over the living room floor.

The poor fish fell out onto the carpet and were flipping around on the floor. He caught the fish in his paw and began to chow down on them.

He didn't take him long to eat half of the fish that were just swimming around in the aquarium.

The light that was on top of the aquarium burned out and broke when the aquarium fell down.

The living room carpet soaked up the water, but the whole floor was saturated. The smell of dead fish filled the living room, he left two dead fish out of ten.

The television in the corner of the room was off, but he still was staring at it. He must of saw his reflection in it and this made him leap straight up in the air.

He landed on top of the coffee table spilling a cup of coffee all over the side of the couch and floor. The coffee must have been there for a while and a bad foul odor

to it.

The nice black leather couch had a brown

coffee stain on it now, he jumped on the

couch and didn't retract his claws and they

got caught in the leathers fabric.

He couldn't move and kept on pulling and

yanking as hard as he could, but he still

couldn't move. His back paws weren't

stuck like his front paws were.

His front paws were really hurting him,

but he couldn't get his sharp claws

unstuck. With his remaining strength, he

pulled on his right foot.

He pulled so hard that treads came out of

the couch, he fell face down onto the

floor. He let out a meow and stood back

up, he sat down on his back legs and watched the curtain near the window.

There was a stink bug slowly crawling along the curtain. Then another one came crawling along.

The one stink bug fell off of the curtain and laid on its back and tried to get back up. There was still one stink bug crawling along, the curtain. Skittles kept on watching, the stink bug just kept on crawling.

He jumped up and tried to catch the stink bug but missed the bug and his long sharp claws got caught on the curtain and he couldn't get his claws uncaught. He pulled down hard and ripped the curtain right off of the wall.

Then he laid down and was exhausted. He put his head down and kept watch, his tail was even caught up in the curtain. He yanked on the curtain hoping that he could get the curtain off of him. He pulled on the curtain ripping it even more, then he was finally able to get himself out of the curtain.

Now he was free again, he was feeling hungry and wandered into the kitchen once again. He walked over to his bowl and ate all of the cat chow and after he finished it he let out a meow.

Meanwhile Harriet was walking along the side of the highway, she saw so many cars coming and going.

Mario came walking back to her and told her that he was done with getting her car on his flat bed.

Oh, thank goodness you have finished up on my car. I thought it was going to take you all afternoon to get the car loaded up. Listen, I'm doing all that I can do. Now climb in the truck and let's go get off of the highway.

"Do you attend college?"

"No," I didn't, I'm too lazy for that.

"How long it is going to take us to get back to the garage?"

It's going to take us exactly twelve minutes to get there If the traffic isn't so bad.

"Are you having a good day today?"

"No," I'm not, and that's enough questions.

All right I'll be quiet and just sit here. After ten more minutes, they reached the garage. All right you can get out now and go and enter the shop.

Harriet walked into the shop and sat down and saw that there was a small table that had a few magazines on it. She saw a home and gardening magazine and picked it up and began to page through it.

The women who was working behind the desk kept watch on Harriet, but she didn't seem to notice.

"How are you doing today? "

"I'm not doing so good today and just want to get out of here."

How about you just Lean back and try to relax Harriet. I will and please be quiet, it seems like you're in a bad mood.

Yes, I'm in a bad mood so just leave me and let me continue on reading this magazine. An hour went by, and Harriet was sleeping sitting up.

Then Mario came into the waiting room and said alright your car is done. It'll be another fifty dollars, for today. Okay Mario, here's the money now let me go.

Have a good rest of the day and if you have another problem with your car call us. I will, bye now.

Harriet got in her car and was now back on her way to her house.

Twenty minutes later she pulled into the driveway and turned her car off. Then she walked into her house and saw that her house was in ruins.

She immediately yelled out and said Skittles I'm going to kill you. Skittles ran out the open door behind Harriet. Get back here you silly cat, you ruined my house.

Skittles kept on running down the street of the neighborhood and missed getting hit by two cars that were coming towards him.

The one car ran over his tail, this caused him to scream out, then another car ran over him and he died five minutes later.

His little body laid in the middle of the street, while cars passed by. Harriet looked all around for Skittles but couldn't find him and soon gave up.

Rudy the People Watcher

On a dark and gloomy Saturday, Rudy rode his skateboard to the Greenwich Mall. He's twenty years old and has been coming to the mall since he was five.

The mall is less than twenty minutes away from his home, him, and his family live in a bi level. His bedroom is on the second floor, there's a living room on the first floor.

His dad is a stockbroker and never has much time to spend with his wife and son.

Each morning his dad wakes up at five o clock in the morning and gets so busy that he sometimes doesn't even eat his breakfast. He doesn't drink alcohol, but he does drink too much soda. His favorite kind of soda is root beer, he doesn't like to eat eggs and usually eats Cheerios or eats pop tarts for breakfast.

He takes a shower at three thirty in the morning. Rudy asks his dad why he takes a shower so early in the morning. His dad says I get so busy and the earlier I get started the quicker I can get to work.

I must be at work by nine o clock in the morning. Your mom is going to be busy today and you can do whatever your heart desires today.

You can either go to the mall or you can just stay home and watch television.

I think that I want to take my skateboard to the mall, just please be careful. I'm just going to be window shopping.

"How much money do you have?"

"I have fifty dollars in my pocket."

I've been cutting the neighbors grass for extra spending money.

"How much do they give you?"

"They give me five dollars, and I never ask for more, and means that you're respecting your elders."

Okay son let me finish up eating my strawberry pop tarts then I have to leave immediately. It always seems like you're in a hurry.

Yes, I am, I'm the one who puts food on the table and pays off all of the debt. I never want to have to be in soup line.

My dad was in a soup line once, and I never want that to happen to me. When you get back from the mall today could you please feed the dog.

"Where are you going to go today?"

"I'm going to the grocery store and should be back in an hour or two. Just drive careful, and I'll talk to you later."

Rudy opened the front door and walked out down the four steps that led out of the front yard. Their dog's name is Soldier, he's a small dog and probably weighs fifteen pounds or less.

He's a Shitzu and always has a good appetite, Rudy likes to pick him and give him a hug every day before he leaves for school.

In the distance he heard some thunder and he looked up and saw that the sky was growing grayer by the minute.

The wind picked up and blew all the leaves around. Some of the trees that he walked past, were full of leaves and other trees had no leaves on them.

He walked along the uneven sidewalk and he heard a Barta bus approaching that was full of elderly people, the driver of the bus looked it he must have been eighty years old. He had so many wrinkles on his forehead with all white hair.

He had a nice smile on his face and waved to Rudy, so he waved back at him. Rudy was wearing a large, orange sweatshirt, and imprinted on the front of the sweatshirt is an image of drums.

His grandmother bought this shirt for him when she was getting ammunition for her shotgun at the ammo shop

Even though his grandmother is up in age, she still likes to go to the range twice a week with her friends.

One time Rudy went with his grandmother to the gun range but after just ten minutes of being at the range he became bored and wanted to text his friends, then decided not to. There were four other friends with his grandmother. She slowly

lifted up her camouflage shotgun and said
release the clay bird.

She took one shot and hit the clay bird
and it blew up and disappeared into the
sky.

Rudy nudged his grandmother on her right
shoulder and said that was some good
shooting grandma. She thanked him and
asked

> "Why don't you take a shot?"

> "No," I don't feel like it, maybe
> another day.

Alright it's all up to you. I was planning on
going home soon Rudy.

> "Would you like me to drive you
> home?"

"Yes," please that would be so nice.

"Is there anything else that I can do for you?"

"No," thanks, but would you please help me to clean my shotgun.

You know I would do anything for you grandma. Yes, I know that. It'll just take me a couple of minutes to clean and oil your shot gun.

"Is that alright? "

"That should be fine. "

It took him twenty-three minutes to finish cleaning and oiling the shotgun. After he was done he carefully placed the shotgun back in her gun case.

Once him and his grandmother got home, his grandmother walked into her living room and bent down and picked up the small controller to her television set.

She clicked the power button, and the television immediately came on. Duck Dynasty was on the television, and it seemed to cause his grandma to perk up.

She said you know son every time that I turn on the television set my favorite show comes on.

"Who's your favorite person on Duck Dynasty?"

"I like uncle Si because he's funny and always cracks me up."

I thought that you were going to say, that your favorite person on the show was Phil. No, he's a bit too wild for my liking.

"Why don't you try to watch a show on the discovery channel?"

"No," that's okay, I like to watch the news too. Rudy got to the mall a little after twelve noon.

There weren't too many people at the mall, all of the stores were open and there were a lot of people upstairs at the food court.

On the second floor of the mall is a McDonald's and a Subway sandwich shop. Rudy prefers to eat at the Subway, he loves to eat tuna fish sandwiches.

But today he wasn't very hungry and wasn't sure if he was going to eat lunch today. He walked on past the Bon Ton and kept on walking past the skateboard shop.

In the middle of the mall was a large dolphin fountain. There were a lot of coins in the fountain.

There was a yellow sign next to the fountain that said slippery when wet. He was careful not to trip.

He walked all the way down the long hallway to the sporting goods store at the other end of the mall.

Today they were running a deal on pellet guns, they had pellet pistols and rifles that had scopes on them.

There weren't many people walking around in the store. He saw a little boy who's shoelaces were untied.

His shoes were the light up kind and said Star Wars on the side of them.

He happened to look off to his left and there was a tall fellow who had a bunch of tattoos on his left and right arms.

He had a blue dragon on his arm and a tattoo of a koi fish on his right arm. Rudy hadn't seen this man before; he didn't see anything that interested him in the store that he was in.

He walked out and sat down on the bench outside of the store. He sat there and watched the people walk past him.

He saw a guy and girl who were holding hands, the girl was carrying a Victoria secret bag. He was carrying a brown bag that was from McDonald's.

After a while he saw a mall security officer and had a real serious look on his face. He had his arms crossed and was shaking his head.

He didn't say anything, but just looked miserable and unhappy. He began to whistle; Rudy could tell that he was in his own little world.

Rudy was getting bored and was thinking about going home, but he was only at the mall for an hour or less.

He got up and carried his skateboard, he quickly walked towards the exit sign in the mall. Within a few minutes he was back outside, it began to down pour down rain. He could tell that it was going to be another long walk home in the down pour.

The Boardwalk Lovers

It was a nice hot sunny day on the boardwalk, it was the beginning of June. Today there were crowds of people walking up and down the long stretch of boardwalk.

Above all the people there were a few seagulls flying around and looking for any kind of food that the people would drop.

On the left side and right side of the boardwalk there were plenty of food stands, some of the food stands were so crowded that it seemed like a live show was going on.

People were leaning over the food stand and the boy standing directly behind the food stand had a look of disgust on his face and had many red freckles on his rosy, red cheeks.

There was a slight ocean breeze, it was just cool enough to feel good. Everyone that had ordered a hot dog also got a side of French fries.

There were a few different kinds of combos that the people could order from the food vender. A couple was sharing a hot dog and some French fries.

The women dropped a French fry and it fell down right in front of her. A sea gull saw the fry and swooped in and scarfed it up and let out a cry as it flew away into the wide-open blue sky.

The couple walked over to the vender and put some ketchup and mustard over there chili dog, the man poured chopped up onions all over the top of the chili dog.

His significant other said to him why must you put so much onion on the top of the hotdog. I love onions and besides that they are good for you.

I was going to kiss you but now I'm not going to until you freshen up your breath.

Hold on Hun while I reach in my purse, I may have one Listerine fresh strip left. She searched around inside her purse and found everything else besides what she was originally looking for.

I can't find what I was looking for, thank you for getting me the chili dog, your welcome honey, anything for you my love.

Hank took a big bite out of the side of the chili dog and handed it to Susan. Now take a bite, I will just let me put my purse back over my shoulder.

Okay but this chili dog is so good and at this rate it's not going to last very long.

Susan carefully took the chili dog from Hank and took a little bite; you know honey you take a bite like a mouse.

"Now why would you say something like that to me?"

"I was just trying to be funny, no you were making fun of me." "Yes," I was but I didn't want to upset you, well you did.

"Are you going to apologize to me?"

"I'm sorry I'll never say that again, alright I forgive you. I'm really getting hungry for French fries."

"Can we order more French fries?"

"Yes," we sure can.

"Would you like a banana split and monkey bread too?"

"No," now don't go crazy now, but I like funnel cake and I can smell it in the air.

You don't have to ask me for permission to get a funnel cake, if you want it then go get it.

"How about if we split up and you go over there and order your funnel cake and I'll go over here and order my French fries?"

"Alright that sounds good, see you soon. The line to get funnel cake was halfway back the whole Boardwalk."

Hank was running low on patience, and he thought to himself should I wait in this line or just wait till tomorrow and come back to the boardwalk.

He happened to look off to his left and saw that the line that Susan was in was much shorter than the line he was in. It was now the middle of the afternoon, Hank reached into left hand into his pocket and began to make the change in his pocket cling around in his pocket.

He could smell the funnel cake aroma once again and this may him feel even more hungry for some funnel cake.

He happened to look towards his left and at a far he could see the Ferris wheel slowly turning and was all lit up.

He loves to watch the Ferris wheel and found himself staring at the Ferris wheel. It was lit up with pretty purple lights.

Every seat on the Ferris wheel was filled up, Hank had a pair of cheap plastic binoculars around his neck.

To see more of the Ferris wheel and to see further along the boardwalk he looked through his binoculars.

He saw a family that was riding on the Ferris wheel, the two children had smiles on their face and one of the children was screaming.

Their father grabbed a hold of his one kids and held him there next to him until he calmed down.

He got tired of looking at the Ferris wheel and looked off to the right of the Ferris wheel and he saw a monster truck, it looked like an exact replica of the grave digger monster truck.

It was so noisy, and a lot of black smoke was coming out of the back of it. He thought well maybe the monster truck had an engine issue.

The truck was just sitting there and wasn't moving, then he saw someone get out of it.

The man that got out of the truck and looked like he was waving to someone that was a few yards away from him. All of a sudden a man walked up to Hank and asked

"Would you like a bag of kettle cooked chips?"

"No," thanks, I'm not hungry for chips, but Sir I'm offering you these chips free of charge.

"Could you please take them?"

"Yes," I will thank you so much for the chips I'll eat them later.

"Why don't you eat them now?"

"No," thank you I'm not hungry right now and I'll save them for later. Alright for as long as you eat the chips Sir.

The man walked away quickly back into the crowd of people. Hank thought this guy was being kind of strange and he didn't want to eat the chips for fear of them being poisoned.

He lifted up his binoculars again and this time looked down at the ocean, there were some big waves that came crashing down onto the beach.

There were young children who were close to where the wave had hit the shore.

He looked further down the beach and saw a lifeguard sitting on a reclined chair texting.

Hank could smell the salty sea air and it smelled good to him. There were plenty of people swimming in the ocean. All of a sudden he heard screams from a far.

Someone was swimming but a big wave caught the person off guard, and they almost drowned in the large ocean wave.

He saw one big wave and there was a yellow surfboard and the man riding the surfboard was crouched down.

He looked like he was going to fall off of the surfboard, Susan slowly walked over to Hank and patted his on his shoulder.

"What are you looking at?"

"I'm sorry, I didn't see you there."

"What were you looking at?"

"I was just looking at the big ocean waves and the monster truck."

"Did you see anything interesting?"

"No," just the usual beach goers.

"Here would you like a nice hot French fry?"

"Yes," I would and thank you very much, you're very welcome.

You forgot to put ketchup on the fries dear, I'm sorry I'll go get some ketchup and be right back. I'm going to help you get the ketchup oh thank you.

He went to put some ketchup over the hot French fries and the ketchup squirted all over his nice orange Hawaiian shirt. Oh, don't worry the ketchup will come off in the washer.

How about we head home after I finish up the pile of French fries. Alright I want to go to the local candy shop on the board

walk and get some saltwater taffy.

"How about if we head over there

now?"

"Yes," but you aren't done eating.

I was going to wait until you were done

eating to go there. No, I these crowds of

people are beginning to really bother me

and besides that I'm tired and would like

to take a nap on the beach.

"Where did you get those bag of

chips?"

"Some strange man had given them

to me and forced me to take them

and eat them. I like kettle cooked

chips."

"Would you mind if I ate them?"

"No," but let's get a move on so that we are home before it gets dark.

I'm going as fast I can, Susan got her saltwater taffy and they walked back to their car and from there drove home.

The Mystery Key

There was a small trailer park, it was called Wilshire trailer park. There was a young man whose name was Casey; he was in his early thirties.

He has two cats and used to have a Yorkshire terrier, but he grew old, and he had to be put down.

Casey loves to study the solar system; he knows a lot about the planets and has studied black holes. His favorite planet is Mars, it's his favorite because water was discovered on Mars.

When he was just a boy he wanted to become an astronaut, but he lost interest in being an astronaut when he turned twenty-two years old.

He has a girlfriend; her name is Lucy. She's thirty-two years old and attends the local college, she's studying to be an Astronomer.

She gets along well with Casey; they have been together for more than five years; they're engaged and are soon planning on getting married.

Casey wants to have one son and a daughter; Lucy just wants to have a son and no daughter. Their trailer home is just big enough for the both of them.

Casey let Lucy decorate the trailer home, she loves flowers and has flowerpots scattered everywhere in the backyard.

In the front yard she has one large flower box, in the flower box there are two different kinds of flowers. The first kind are daisies, the second kind are purple mums.

She makes sure that she waters them every day. She's planning on making a sand box for her son when she has him.

Casey let Lucy paint the inside of the trailer. She painted the inside walls of the trailer a tan color, it was mid-July, and it was eighty degrees outside.

Casey opened the bedroom window, and there was a cool breeze going. Lucy was at school; he was home all alone.

He was so bored today and just could not find anything to occupy his time, so he wandered around his backyard and heard a woodpecker pecking away at the old oak tree.

One of the branches of the tree fell down right in front of Casey. He bent over and picked up the branch and threw it out of the yard.

This caused the woodpecker to fly away. He looked up at the telephone pole and saw a gray squirrel climbing up the pole.

Above the pole was a long black wire, there were four little birds perched there. Casey just happened to remember that it was going to be a full moon that night.

He forgot to get his telescope ready for the night, so he walked back into his trailer and got his telescope out of its case. He quickly assembled the telescope.

He was missing an important part that kept the tri pod legs together, he dug through the case and still couldn't find the part.

He was getting frustrated and decided to look on the shelf next to his small bed.

There were a lot of baseball figures on the shelf and each one had a layer of dust on them.

He began to cough when he went to lift up the baseball figures. He doesn't have allergies, but a lot of dust causes him to sneeze.

There was a Mets baseball cap hanging up on the wall, he went to lift it up and a few stink bugs came flying out.

One of them landed on his shoulder and another one landed in his hair, he went crazy trying to get the one stink bug out his hair.

He ran all around the small room trying to get the stink bug out of his hair.

His arms were flaring all around, the stink bug eventually flew off of his head and landed on his bed.

He didn't like that it landed there and tried to hit it with a fly swatter, he missed and was now so irritated.

The stink bug crawled away from his bed and crawled onto the wall to the left of the bed.

On the ceiling Casey had a poster of a fancy sports car. He loves Lamborghinis and if he had the money he would go buy one.

On the far wall there was a Phillies baseball clock, Lucy's dad had bought her the clock two years ago for her birthday.

Casey decided to look under the bed and there the piece was that went to his telescope stand.

He was so happy that he jumped up and down and yelled out yes I finally found it.

He went back over to the telescope and put the piece into the main stand. He went to look through his telescope and there was some dust on the main lens.

He quickly grabbed a roll of paper towels from the nightstand, and a cup of water and placed two paper towels in the water and began to wipe the lens off.

He took a quick look through the lens and now could see more clearly. The sky was filled with clouds today, there were some fast-moving clouds and they appeared to be black rain clouds.

He saw one cloud that reminded him of a shark. He stopped looking through the telescope and turned around, and happened to look out his window and he saw a black bear walking through his backyard, he was so surprised to see a bear.

He couldn't believe what he was seeing.
All of a sudden the sun light shined
through his window and nearly blinded
him, so he quickly found a pair of
sunglasses and slipped them.

The bear stood up on its hind legs and
sniffed the air and sat back down onto its
all fours.

He was so heavy set and it seemed to be
a pregnant mother bear, who was going
to have her cub soon.

The bear remained rummaging around his
back yard for almost a half an hour. There
was an old coffee can sitting by the door
of his trailer.

The bear walked over to the can and
crushed the can and began to sniff it. He

watched as she walked into his front yard, where he had a bird bath, that was full of water.

The bear seemed to be thirsty and stood up on its back legs and began to take a drink out of the bird bath, but the bird bath couldn't support her weight and flipped over to its side.

Ten minutes later the bear wandered out of the yard, he went out to the front yard and stood the bird bath back up.

He happened to look down and saw a strange looking golden key. The key didn't look familiar to him, and he put it in his left side pocket.

The key slid down to the bottom of his deep pocket. He walked back into the trailer and sat down at the small folding table.

He took the key back out of his pocket and placed it on the table, for he wanted to take a closer look at it.

He closely examined it and couldn't find any numbers, or anything written on the key. He opened a drawer and took out a magnifying glass and looked the key over again.

He thought to himself when maybe Lucy will know what it belongs to. He looked down at his cell phone and it went off.

He picked it up and said hello. It was Lucy, how are you doing? I'm doing good, I'm in the bathroom right now, I just wanted to quick call and see how you were doing. You won't believe it but there was a mother black bear in our backyard.

It had gone into the front yard and knocked down the bird bath, I went out to stand it back up and I found a small gold key on the ground beneath it.

"Do you know who or what the key belongs to?"

"No," why don't you call your dad and ask him, it might be to our safety security box at the bank. I think you may be right, that was easy

"Do you have any other questions for me?"

"No," I don't.

"What have you been doing at

home?"

"I got my telescope ready for

tonight, oh yeah that's right tonight

a full moon."

How about we have a romantic kind of

evening and share a glass of white wine

and we can celebrate our great life

together.

"When are you going to be home

this evening?"

"I should be home at five o clock."

"Is there anything that you want me

to pick up for you at the local

grocery store? "

"No," thank you, and so I have to get back to class before the teacher wonders where I am.

Have a good rest of the day and I'll talk to you later tonight. Okay bye now, I love you Casey, I love you too Lucy.

They hung up and he placed his phone back in his pocket and got his cars keys and took the mystery key with him. He got in his car and drove down to the local Post Office.

Within ten minutes he was pulling into the parking lot. He got out of his car and slowly walked into the bank; it took him a moment to find his safety security box.

He took the key out of his pocket and tried it and it opened the box. He was amazed and had a big smile on his face.

All of a sudden a tall full-figured man walked in behind him and wasn't looking where he was walking and almost walked right into him.

Casey turned around and said watch where your walking next time. The man said I'm sorry, and it won't happen again.

He put his safety security box back and left the small post office and returned home.

The Watermelon Eater

One day there was a young girl whose name was Emily. She was fifteen years old; she was always spending time with her grandmother.

Her grandmother loves to eat fruit, when her grandmother was young she used to live on a farm. On the farm they grew wild strawberries and watermelons.

The watermelon plants grew better than the strawberry plants and she could not figure out why.

Her grandmother is now aged ninety-three, Emily doesn't always listen to her grandma and her grandmother loves to watch movies with her. Her grandmothers name is Tammy. Emily likes to eat desert and doesn't like to eat her vegetables.

Tammy is always trying to get Emily to eat her vegetables and puts ranch dressing on her broccoli but still turns her nose up at it. One day Tammy said to Emily you're lucky that you weren't me back then.

"Why's that?"

"When I was a kid I wasn't allowed to leave the table until I ate all of my vegetables, I learned to like my vegetables."

"What kind of vegetables did you used to have to eat?"

"I would have to eat green beans and cauliflower."

If you eat your vegetables you'll grow up strong, I have heard that before grandma. Please don't be rude to me I was talking to you, and you interrupted me.

"Can I go swimming?"

"Yes," you can but I'm going to watch you, and make sure nothing bad happens to you.

I'm a good swimmer and I don't think that I'm going to drown. I'm getting thirsty, I would like some lemonade.

You're so demanding today and your mom and dad said that they're going to come back at six o clock tonight and it's just going on one o clock in the afternoon. I'm going to change into my bathing suit, I'll be right out. Take your time.

Within a few minutes Emily came out of the bathroom and said alright I'm going to jump in the pool. Now no running into the pool, don't worry I'll be fine.

Emily slowly bent down and got into the pool. She grabbed onto a noodle, and she leaned forward onto the noodle and began to kick her legs. She kicked and splashed, and water went everywhere.

She was feeling relaxed and kept on splashing around in the pool. Then all of a sudden she dived down to the bottom of the pool and held her breath. Then she returned to the surface and her grandma said to her

"What were you doing at the bottom of the pool?"

"I was just relaxing, you call that relaxing, you had me scared and I was going to jump into the pool and save you."

It's alright, I wasn't drowning. I know that, but I love you and don't want anything to happen to you. Come on why don't you jump in the pool with me.

Maybe later, I need to do some gardening after you get out of the pool.

"How much longer do you want to swim for?"

"I want to swim for another hour or so."

That's a good thing and you're getting your exercise. I like to exercise, I'm happy you like to swim.

I'm going to be right back; I'm going to bring out some lemonade. Ten minutes later her grandma came out.

"Are you alright?"

"Yes," I'm just enjoying swimming around.

Grandma handed her a glass of lemonade. Thanks, and she took a big sip of lemonade. That's some really good lemonade and now I'm going back to swimming.

All of a sudden a swarm of bees came flying into the backyard. Emily watch out here comes some bees, and Emily quickly dunked down under the water.

Emily was watching her grandma from under the water and saw that there were three yellow jackets buzzing around her head.

She tried to open up her back door, but her hand slipped off the handle and one of the bees stung her on the arm. She yelled out and eventually was able to get the door open and ran inside.

Emily rose up out of the water and saw a bee and began to splash at it. The bee quickly flew off, and she was relieved.

Emily was so upset about what she had just saw happened to her grandma. She walked up the steps and got out of the pool, although it was so burning hot outside. Within a couple of minutes her skin was turning red from the hot sun.

She opened the door and yelled inside, and her grandmother said hold on just a minute. I'm carving up a watermelon and I'll be out in just a moment.

Emily sat down in a lawn chair and sprayed her body with some more sunscreen. The umbrella wasn't opened and there was no shade.

It must have been eighty-two degrees outside and now the sweat was pouring down her face.

She didn't like that she was sweating so much, she was thinking to herself and thought I think that I want to go back in the pool.

She slowly stepped back into the pool, and the cold water felt so good. Her body cooled down and she was no longer sweating.

She dunked her head down into the cold water and immediately felt refreshed.

Then after a few minutes her grandma
came walking out with a large white tray,
it had a watermelon cut in half on it.

Emily kept on swimming and didn't notice,
what her grandma had brought out.

"Why don't you come out of the
pool and enjoy some watermelon
with me?"

"Yes," I would, and she walked out
of the pool.

I think that you should come inside soon,
or you're going to get a serious burn. But
I just sprayed on more suntan lotion.

"How's the watermelon?"

"It tastes great"

"Can I have some more?"

"You sure can."

Emily took another piece of watermelon and let out a burp. I don't like the little black seeds in the watermelon.

Stop complaining, at least you're able to eat good food. That's true, and I'm sorry that I complained about the seeds. Why must watermelon have seeds; I actually don't know why.

I thought you knew everything. No, I don't all there's to know. Oh, but you're still a good grandma and I love you.

I love you too and she smiled and giggled, I wish that my grandpa was still alive I miss him so very much.

A tear ran down the side of Emily's face and she said I can still remember all the good times that we had together with grandpa. We did have some great memories together and we will never forget them.

I can still remember when grandpa took us out to the lake, I had caught my first fish. I can barely remember what kind of fish it was; I remember grandma.

"What kind of fish was it?"

"It was a trout, and it was kind of small."

"Is that all that you can remember about the fish?"

"Yes," it is, but most of all I loved grandpas smile.

He always knew how to cheer me up when I was feeling bad, I remember his smile and I miss him very much. I look at his picture every day and it makes me smile.

I hope that you stay healthy and are here for a while and not going anywhere. I love you so much and they gave each other a big hug, your body feels really hot.

I think that it's time that we go inside and don't talk back at me. I'm behaving, and I'm learning to be more respectful.

You have good parents; I love all of you with all my heart. Her grandma was eating watermelon and all of a sudden her false teeth got stuck in the watermelon.

"What happened to your teeth?"

"It's alright, sometimes when you
get older you lose your teeth."

I hope that I don't lose my teeth when I'm
your age, just make sure that you always
brush your teeth good.

"Did it hurt to lose all of your
teeth?"

"Yes," it was very painful.

I have had three root canals and I have
had a tooth drilled. My goodness grandma
you have been through a lot.

It's a good thing that you like brushing
your teeth.

"Does watermelon rot your teeth?"

"Why would you ask me a question
like that?"

"I was just curious, and I like to learn things grandma."

I didn't mean to upset you it's okay.

"Would you like to watch something on television?"

"No," I don't feel like sitting down.

"Why's that?"

"Did your parents give you too much candy today?"

"No," I didn't have any candy today.

I don't want any candy, just let me alone. That's no way to talk to your grandmother.

Now let's try to settle down and be nice to each other. I want to take a walk around the block and see if my friends are hanging around. I'm sorry, but I think that it's too hot for you outside.

It's not ninety degrees, it's probably just eighty-four degrees. Would you please just listen to me and stop giving me so many problems.

I never start an argument with you, but you always start one with me. I'm tired Emily and I want to rest and watch some television.

That's not fair to me, you're just thinking of yourself and that's it. Oh, you're going to drive me to drink. You have been bothering me all day about being outside.

Okay if you want to go, then I'll have to go with you and make sure that you stay safe. Alright let's go now, I have to go into my bedroom and grab my sun visor hat, I'll be right back.

Within a few minutes she came back and was wearing a pink sun visor and sunglasses.

You like your hats, it's not because I like them it's because they help to protect my head from getting bad sun burn.

I have to take a special medicine and it makes me more likely to get a bad sun burn.

"Why's there a black and blue mark on your right arm?"

"The other day I was out gardening, and I bumped my arm on a bucket and it left a mark."

When you get as old as I am it's easy to get a black and blue mark or just a bruise. I'm sorry that you got another mark on your arm.

It's okay I'll be okay, and it'll heal up. So, they walked out front, they saw some people on bicycles slowly going by. They were all teenagers, one of the looked at Emily and disappeared down the street. Grandma looked at Emily

"Who was that boy?"

"I don't know who that was"

"Are you sure?"

"Yes," I'm sure. You know it wouldn't be good if you kept secrets from me.

I realize that, but I wouldn't keep a secret from you. I love you and I don't act shady like that.

As they began to walk down the sidewalk they saw an elderly man walking his dog down the street.

Then a young woman was jogging past the dog and his dog jumped up and tried to bite her. She just ran off and ran across someone yards to get away from the dog.

The dog didn't seem to like her very much, the old man pulled on his dogs lease and said what were you trying to do you dumb dog.

Now sit down, I need to have a talk with you. It was like he was expecting the dog to say something back to him. The dog

just let out a whimper and put his head
down.

Sunny I can't let you behave this way; you
know it's not okay to bite or chase people.
Tonight, I'm not going to give you a
biscuit.

You're a bad dog and I know you know
what I'm saying to you. Emily couldn't
understand why the old man was taking
so much time talking to his dog.

It seems like everyone is out today, but
it's not going to ruin our fun. Now come
on let's go further down the block.

"Can we please stop by the ice
cream truck and get some ice
cream?"

"Only if he comes along."

The ice cream truck doesn't come to our block every day though.

"Do you think he's going to come along here soon?"

"I don't think that he's going to come by today."

"Why can't you be just a bit more positive and not so negative."

"Do you think he gets paid to give us ice cream?"

"He does, you can't expect someone to work and not pay them.

They walked past an old man who was sitting in a lawn chair. "He had a beer in his hand and seemed like he was sleeping.

He was wearing an old hat that said
Oldsmobile on it. He must have been a fan
of Oldsmobile; he had a Navy tattoo on his
arm, on the folding table next to him was
a pack of cigarettes. Emily thought to
herself what a dirty old man, I'm glad that
he's not my grandfather.

"What are you looking at?"

"I was looking at the old man"

"Why were you looking at him?"

"I like to look at new people."

You're such a curious child; these days
you can't be too curious. We have reached
the end of the block, now let's go back.

"Do we have to walk past that
elderly man again?"

"Yes," I'm afraid we do.

"Do you know his name?"

"No," I don't, I don't care either.

Let's just go and forget about him.

"How long has he been in the
neighborhood for?"

"He's been here for forty years."

"Have you ever talked to him?"

"Yes," I have

He was kind and considerate to me, we
are almost back to the house. You know
it's so hot outside, it's hard enough for me
to breath.

Thank goodness were back at my house. Let's get inside and cool off, just as they were walking into her house.

Emilie's parents pulled up into the driveway, your parents are over an hour early.

"Did you enjoy your time with me?"

"I sure did; you're the best."

Now give me a big hug and I'll talk to you later, she waved as she was walking away.